First published in the United States, Great Britain, Canada,
Australia and New Zealand in 1987 by North-South Books, an
imprint of Rada Matija AG.

Distributed in the United States by
Henry Holt and Company, Inc., 521 Fifth Avenue,
New York, New York 10175.
Library of Congress Cataloging in Publication Data

Scheidl, Gerda Marie.
Four candles for Simon.

Translation of: Die vier Lichter des Hirten Simon.
Summary: A nine-year-old shepherd boy searching for a
missing lamb encounters several individuals less fortunate
than he before eventually making a miraculous discovery of
a newborn baby in a stable.
[1. Shepherds--Fiction   2. Jesus Christ--Nativity--
Fiction.   3. Christmas--Fiction]   I. Pfister, Marcus, ill.
II. Title.
PZ7.S3429Fo   1987   [E]   86-33199

ISBN 0-8050-0494-7

Distributed in Great Britain by
Blackie and Son Ltd, 7 Leicester Place,
London WC2H 7BP.
British Library Cataloguing in Publication Data

Scheidl, Gerda Marie
Four candles for Simon.
I. Title   II. Pfister, Marcus   III. Die
vier Lichter des Hirten Simon. *English*
833'.914[J]   PZ7

ISBN 0-200-72913-6

Distributed in Canada by
Editions Etudes Vivantes, Saint-Laurent.

Distributed in Australia and New Zealand by
Buttercup Books Pty. Ltd., Melbourne.
ISBN 0 949447 58 7

Printed in Germany

Four Candles for Simon

A Christmas story by Gerda Marie Scheidl
Translated by Anthea Bell
Illustrated by Marcus Pfister

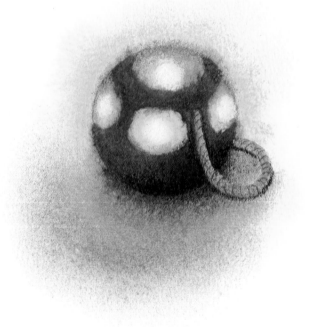

North-South Books

Two thousand years ago, a little shepherd boy called Simon was keeping watch over sheep in the distant land of Galilee.

The day was grey, and heavy mists covered the land.

Abdon, the owner of the flock, looked up to the sky, but there was no sign of the sun. So he sent his shepherds Jacob and Simon to pastures farther up in the hills where his sheep could graze above the mists.

Simon kept close to Jacob, because the thick mist made him feel uneasy. Simon was still quite small, only nine years old, but Jacob was big and strong. He put a protective arm round Simon's shoulders.

Then a lamb as white as snow came running towards them, bleating anxiously. Jacob picked the lamb up and put it in Simon's arms. "Here," he said. "You must carry our smallest lamb. Take good care of it."

Simon was glad to look after the lamb, and didn't let it out of his sight. He even let it sleep under his coat at night, which made him and the lamb both feel warm and safe.

Jacob and Simon stayed up in the hills for six days, until it was time to round up the sheep and drive them home. The grass here had all been grazed, and Abdon would have to find new pastures.

Simon was going to help Jacob, but Jacob shook his head. "You and the lamb had better rest while I round up the sheep."

Simon was glad. The lamb had led him on quite a chase, always running away and having to be caught again. So he sat down under an olive tree and closed his tired eyes while the lamb snuggled up to him.

Then Simon smelled a wonderful fragrance, a scent of roses, lilies, and almond blossoms. He tried to open his eyes, but his lids were too heavy. He thought he could hear joyful singing too. It became clearer and clearer, and then, suddenly there was silence. The sweet scent was gone as well.

When Simon managed to open his eyes at last, he saw Jacob standing over him. "Where is the lamb?" asked Jacob, looking gravely at Simon.

Simon was horrified. The lamb had been there with him only a moment ago! He jumped up and called it. But the lamb's familiar bleating did not answer him. He looked everywhere, but could not find it.

"Come on, we must drive the flock home," said Jacob.

Simon walked sadly along beside the sheep. Where was his lamb? Had any harm come to it? What would Abdon say?

Abdon was not at all pleased when Simon told him the lamb was lost.

"This tale of yours about a wonderful dream is sheer nonsense!" said Abdon crossly. "You went to sleep instead of keeping watch!" Angrily, he shook Simon by the shoulders. "You must set out to search for my lamb at once, and don't you dare come back without it!" he threatened.

Jacob did not think the boy should set off all
alone, but he could not go against his master's
orders. So he went to his room and fetched a
lantern with four candles in it. A traveller had
once given him the lantern, telling him, "If a man
is ever in trouble, this light will shine in his
darkness."

Now Jacob gave the lantern to Simon, saying,
"Take care of these four candles, and they will
light your way."

Simon took the lantern with the four candles,
and they flared up brightly in his hands. He set
off with hope in his heart to look for his lamb.

Simon had been searching the hills all day and all night, but he had found no trace of his lost lamb.

The sun was sinking again. Should he go on looking? Surely his search was pointless!

But wasn't that something moving over there, behind a rock? Was it his lamb?

"Lamb, come here, little lamb!" begged Simon hopefully.

"Hey there!" growled a man's deep voice. "What are you looking for? A lamb, did you say?"

Simon saw a tall man standing in front of him. He was scared, and wanted to run away.

"No need to run away from me," said the man. "But if it's a lamb you're searching for, you'll find it in the olive grove beyond that rock. I saw it there. A little, snow-white lamb."

"That's my lamb!" cried Simon happily. "You found my lamb! Oh, thank you! Can I do anything to help you in return?"

"Help me? No one can help me. My path lies in darkness," said the man, quietly.

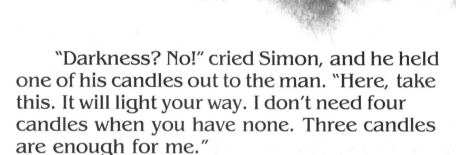

"Darkness? No!" cried Simon, and he held one of his candles out to the man. "Here, take this. It will light your way. I don't need four candles when you have none. Three candles are enough for me."

"You're giving me a candle? Me?" said the amazed man as he took the candle. "You are the first person who has ever been friendly to me. Thank you. Thank you, my boy." And as he went away the man whispered to himself, "Friendly to me, a thief."

Night had fallen now, and Simon ran to the olive grove to find his lamb.

But there was no sign of the lamb. Was it hiding?
Simon saw something moving in a cave, and ran
to look. Was it his lamb? No, it was a wolf! The
wolf snapped at Simon's coat. Shaking with fear,
Simon tried to pull his coat away.

 The wolf immediately let go. It was whining
and licking its paw.

Only then did Simon see that the wolf's paw was hurt and bleeding. All his fear was gone. Quickly, he tore a piece off his coat and carefully bound up the wound.

"Now, you must be a good wolf and lie there until your wound has healed," Simon said.

He rose, to go searching for his lamb again, but the wolf tugged at his coat once more, gazing at him.

"Do you want me to stay with you? Is that what you're trying to say?" Simon stroked the wolf. "But I can't do that. I have to look for my lamb. It may need my help, just as you did."

He thought for a little while, and then he put one of his candles down beside the wolf. "Here you are, wolf," said Simon. "This candle is for you. It will keep you warm. Two candles are enough for me. Jacob will understand." The wolf looked grateful as he watched him go.

But where was Simon to
look for the lamb now? He
wandered around for hours,
and at daybreak he came to a little town. As he
walked down the street, he met an old beggar.
"Give me something, just something small!"
called the man.

"I'm afraid I have nothing myself," said
Simon, stopping. "I'm only a poor shepherd, and
I've lost my lamb!"

"A lamb?" asked the beggar.

"Yes, it ran away from me. Have you seen it?"

"No, all I have seen is hunger and misery," replied the old man. "I live outside the town with the poorest of the poor, in a cold, dark cave."

"Then take this candle, at least," said Simon. "It will give you light and a little warmth. I have nothing else," he added.

The old man took the candle and stood up. "Thank you, and I hope you find your lamb soon."

And so they went their separate ways.

Simon had asked all around the little town, but no one had seen his lamb. He began to lose hope, and the light of his last candle was very faint now. When night fell he sat wearily down by the roadside outside the town.

Just then the same wonderful fragrance settled all around him, the scent of roses, lilies and almond blossoms.

Where did the delightful fragrance come from?
As Simon rose to his feet, he could hear the
joyful singing again. He looked around.
    Then he saw light inside a stable. He walked
towards it, hesitated, and went in.

Simon could scarcely see anything at first. He stood there, blinking.

Then he saw something white shimmering in the dim light inside the stable. It was his lamb, his own lost lamb!

"Come closer," said a kindly voice. Simon could not reply; he was so happy. And then he saw the baby, lying in the straw beside his snow-white lamb.

Simon knelt down and gave the baby his last candle. The flame burnt very faintly. But how strange! It flared up again, as if kindled by an invisible hand, and the shining light spread, filling the room with a radiant glow.

The stars in the sky shone brighter and brighter, and the joyful song rang out to the shepherds keeping watch over their flocks in the fields.